The white, crane-shaped blossoms that arrive in late spring are long gone. All summer the vines have grown in sandy soil. Now they hang heavy with berries. The cool autumn winds have turned them a rich red color that means it's time to start harvesting, time for cranberries.

Time *for* Cranberries

Lisl H. Detlefsen   *Illustrated by* Jed Henry

Roaring Brook Press
New York

Dad's pickup truck *thumps* and *bumps* down the road.
Mom and I bounce in the backseat as he drives through our cranberry marsh.
It's harvesttime and I'm finally old enough to help.

Dad asks, "Are you ready, Sam?"

"Yes!" We hop out and our waders *shlip* and *shlerp* in the mud.

The first beds where the cranberry vines grow have
been flooded for picking.
The tips of the vines peek out from shallow water.

Dad steers the picking machine straight down the length of the bed.
Trails of berries *hop* and *pop* up behind him.

"When can we eat them?" I ask.

"When we're done harvesting," Mom says. "Now, it's time for booming."

We keep flooding the picked bed until the vines are completely covered and the berries bob on the water.

We pull the boom off a giant spool and it *slaps* and *flaps* the water as we toss it in.

The foam-filled boom floats, just like the cranberries.

I climb into one tractor with Dad, and Mom drives the other.
As the tractors move, the boom collects the cranberries.
I watch to make sure we catch every single one.

"Time for eating?" I ask.

"Not yet," Dad says. "Time for corralling."

We wade in, *huffing* and *puffing* as we lasso
the cranberries.
The wet boom zooms through my hands.
I *slide* and *slip*.

Water rushes into my waders
and down to my toes.

As I fall, Dad pulls me back up and hollers, "Time for splashing!"
Mom laughs as she sprays Dad with a wet blast of berries.
We *splish* and *splash* until the autumn air makes me shiver.

Dad lifts me out of the bed and I squish
back to the pickup.

"I always say you're not a cranberry
grower until you fall in," Dad says.

I have to change into dry clothes, but cranberry growers like me don't mind.
You need to be prepared for everything when it's time for harvest.

We continue corralling the cranberries into one big bunch called a pot.

I need every bit of my super strength to help Dad heave the boom against the weight of all those berries.

As we tighten the boom, two spinning paddles push the cranberries to the suction pump and into the cleaner.

"Time for cleaning," Mom says.
We climb the ladder to the top of the cleaner.
Bright berries *bounce* and *boogie* down the
metal grates.

I check the spray bars to make sure the water pushes every bad berry and cranberry leaf through the grates and down to the trash truck.

The good cranberries fall into the delivery truck and pile higher and higher.

"Look at all those cranberries!" I say. "Is it time for eating now?"

"Almost," Dad says. "But first it's time for delivery."

While Dad drives down the highway, I pull the cord to blare the horn.
The other drivers honk back and wave along the way.

At the receiving station, the smell of fresh cranberries fills the air.

The truck tips and our fruit pours out, flooding the pool with billions of berries.

I can't wait any longer.

I reach in and grab a handful.

My lips pucker as I *crunch* and *munch*
the tart and tangy fruit.
"Finally," I say. "Time for eating."

Day after day and week after week we harvest.
As the last leaves fall, we deliver our final
truckloads of cranberries.

One frosty morning, I follow
my nose to the kitchen.

The oven door *clangs* and *bangs* as Mom takes out cranberry pies.
"Yes!" I cheer. "Time for Thanksgiving."

I love every season on our marsh, but I think fall will always be my favorite.

For cranberry growers like me, fall means it's time for cranberries.

Grandma's Homemade Cranberry Sauce

Whether you like whole berry or jellied, all sauce starts with sugar, water, and cranberries.

> *3 cups of fresh or frozen cranberries*
> *1 cup of water*
> *1 cup of sugar*

Mix the sugar and water in a medium saucepan and bring it to a boil. Add the cranberries and bring it to a boil again. Lower the heat and simmer until the berries "pop" (about 10 minutes), stirring occasionally.

For whole berry sauce: Allow the mixture to cool at room temperature and then cover and refrigerate until serving.

For jellied sauce: Put a wire mesh strainer over a medium-sized mixing bowl. Pour the cranberry mixture into the strainer. Mash the cranberries with the back of a large spoon and push all of the cranberry pulp through the strainer. (You can also use a food mill, like you would for applesauce.) Stir the strained sauce in the mixing bowl and pour into a serving bowl. Allow the mixture to cool at room temperature and then cover and refrigerate until serving.

Aunt Kristen's Cranberry Pie

In our family, no Thanksgiving meal is complete without this cakelike cranberry pie.

> *3 cups of cranberries, cut in half*
> *½ cup of brown sugar*
> *1 pie crust for a 10-inch pie pan*
> *2 eggs*
> *1 cup of white sugar*
> *1 cup of flour*
> *½ cup of melted butter*
> *Aluminum foil*

Mix the cranberries and brown sugar together and spread evenly in the bottom of the unbaked pie crust. Using an electric mixer, beat the eggs well. Add the white sugar and beat until well combined. Mix in the flour and melted butter, adding a little of each at a time. Spread the batter (it will be thick) over the cranberry mixture in the pie crust. Cover the crust edges with aluminum foil and bake at 400 degrees for 15 minutes. Then place foil over the whole pie, turn the oven down to 350 degrees, and bake for 45–50 minutes. Remove all of the aluminum foil and bake uncovered for the last 5 minutes, or until the batter is set and the top is golden brown. Serve plain or with a scoop of vanilla ice cream.

Author's Note

Nestled in the heart of Wisconsin is my home on the Whittlesey cranberry marsh. My husband's great-great-grandfather bought the original section of land from the state of Wisconsin in 1871. In 1956, our marsh joined Ocean Spray and we are proud to sell all of our fruit through this grower-owned cooperative.

The cranberry is one of North America's few native fruits, and more cranberries are grown in Wisconsin than in any other state. In fact, Wood County, the county where our marsh is located, has one of the highest amounts of cranberry acreage in the world. Cranberries are also grown in Massachusetts, New Jersey, Oregon, Washington, Canada, and even Chile.

Cranberry harvesting is a unique process and every marsh uses a slightly different method to get the job done. *Time for Cranberries* depicts our process for harvesting fruit used to make juice, sauce, and dried cranberries. However, our friends just ten miles down the road use different picking machines and boats to take their cranberries out of the beds instead of a suction pump. Their cranberries are then sorted and bagged on-site to be sold as fresh fruit in stores.

Life on our marsh has changed a lot since 1871. Back then, cranberries were picked with special rakes and cleaned and sorted by hand. Thanks to new innovations, what used to take dozens of workers several months to harvest can now be done with eight workers in three weeks. But it still takes everybody working together, like the family in this book, when it's time for cranberries.

Glossary

bed: an area of land that cranberries grow in, typically shaped like a rectangle

boom: long floating tubes filled with foam used to corral cranberries

booming: the gathering of picked floating cranberries at one end of the bed

cleaner: metal grates and spray bars used to clean and separate the good cranberries from the bad berries and leaves

corralling: the moving of cranberries toward the suction pump

delivery truck: vehicle used to collect and transport harvested cranberries from the marsh to the receiving station

marsh: word used to describe the entire cranberry farm; also called a bog

picking machine: a machine that removes the cranberries from the vines

pot: term for the cranberries collected during the corralling process

receiving station: where the cranberries are taken to be cleaned and inspected for size and color

suction pump: a machine that draws the cranberries out of the cranberry bed and up into the cleaner

tractor: a farm vehicle used to pull the boom during cranberry harvest

trash truck: a dump truck used for collecting bad berries and cranberry leaves

waders: tall, waterproof boots, pants, or overalls worn to keep warm and dry while in the water

For Robert

This book is my love letter to you, our family, and the cranberry community
—LHD

Library of Congress Cataloging-in-Publication Data
Detlefsen, Lisl H.
    Time for cranberries / Lisl H. Detlefsen ; illustrated by Jed Henry.
        pages   cm
    Summary: Sam is finally old enough to help his parents harvest cranberries on their family
farm, from flooding the field to prepare the vines for the picking machine to delivering the
fruit to receiving station. Includes recipes for cranberry sauce and cranberry pie, author's
note, and glossary.
    ISBN 978-1-62672-098-5 (hardback)
    [1. Cranberries—Fiction. 2. Harvesting—Fiction. 3. Farm life—Wisconsin—Fiction.]
    I. Henry, Jed, illustrator. II. Title.
    PZ7.1.D478Tim 2015
    [E]–dc23

2015003615

Roaring Brook Press books may be purchased for business or promotional use.
For information on bulk purchases please contact Macmillan Corporate and Premium Sales
Department at (800) 221-7945 x5442 or by email at specialmarkets@macmillan.com.

First edition 2015
Book design by Andrew Arnold
Printed in China by RR Donnelly Asia Printing Solutions Ltd., Dongguan City, Guangdong Province

1   3   5   7   9   10   8   6   4   2